MIKE'S GANG

MIKE'S GANG

Rosemary Weir

Illustrated by
Charles Pickard

Abelard-Schuman
London   New York   Toronto

By the same author
Mike's Gang
No sleep for Angus
Pyewacket

© Rosemary Weir 1965
First Published 1965
Reprinted 1966
Library of Congress Catalogue Card Number: 65-14718
ISBN: 0 200 71264 0

Weekly Reader Children's Book Club Edition

LONDON	NEW YORK	TORONTO
Abelard-Schuman	*Abelard-Schuman*	*Abelard-Schuman*
Limited	*Limited*	*Canada Limited*
8 King St.	*257 Park Ave. So.*	*228 Yorkland Blvd.*
WC2	*10010*	*425*

Contents

1 : Mike   9

2 : Tizzy   25

3 : Boston Bill   39

4 : Shep   53

5 : The Twins   69

6 : Prince   84

7 : The Raid   97

8 : Hopes and Homes   111

1 : Mike

A mongrel, that is what Mike was. He had a grey, shaggy coat, a cairn terrier's head with prick ears, long legs, and a beautiful tail which curved gracefully over his back. He was a comic who made you smile to look at him, but he was a nice comic, with a kind, intelligent expression in his dark brown eyes.

Mike sometimes wondered if perhaps his mother had been a pure bred cairn. He didn't know, because he couldn't remember her at all. As soon as Mike was able to lap milk out of a saucer, he and his two brothers and sister were taken away and put up for sale on a pet stall in a street market in London. There they sat in a box of dirty straw, waiting for people to buy them. The other three puppies whined and cried unhappily for their mum, but Mike sat silently, watching everyone who went by and wondering what would happen next.

What did happen was that his brothers and his sister, who were better looking than he, were all

sold, and Mike was left alone in the dirty box until evening drew on and the street lamps flicked into golden stars.

"Dratted nuisance being left with just the one," thought the stall keeper crossly. "He'll yowl all night if he's on his own. Reckon I'd better sell him off cheap."

"How cheap?" asked Mike anxiously, but the man didn't answer because, of course, humans don't understand dogs, although dogs very often understand them. In any case, he had just turned away to speak to a big, shabby boy who was poking at some rabbits in a cage.

"Leave them rabbits be!" the man said sharply.

"All right, I was only looking," replied the big boy sulkily. "No harm in that, is there?" He stared around the stall, at the kittens and the guinea pigs and the birds, and sniffed.

"I wanted a little dorg," he said. "But you ain't got none left."

"Yes I have though," said the stall keeper quickly. "A lovely little dorg. Pure bred. Thirty shillings and he's yours."

"Oh, go on!" said the boy, peering into the box

11

at Mike, who stared boldly back again. "He's not pure bred and you know it. What's more he don't look old enough to leave his mum."

"He eats lovely," said the stall keeper defiantly. "Do you want him or don't you? He's yours for a quid."

"Five bob," said the boy, lifting Mike out of the box and looking him over carefully. "That's all I've got, so I can't give you no more."

"Oh, all rignt," said the stall keeper. "It's giving him away, but I'm glad for him to have a good home."

"How do you know it'll be a good home?" asked Mike, doubtfully. He wasn't stupid even though he was only five weeks old.

"Listen to him growling!" said the boy admiringly. "He's a proper little tyke."

"Show us your money," said the stall keeper, and the boy took two half-crowns out of his pocket and handed them over. Then he tucked Mike inside his coat and walked away.

"Now what?" said Mike to himself. He felt very small and lonely and thought longingly of his dear, furry mum. But he didn't whine or cry because he wasn't that sort. He just kept quiet and waited for the next thing to happen.

The boy walked for some time and then he caught a bus and then he walked again. At last he came to a small, mean-looking house, in a dark, narrow, smelly street, opened the door and went in.

"So you're back at last," said a woman's voice. "Well, did you get the job?"

Mike poked his head out of the boy's coat and looked around. He saw a small room with a popping gas fire and a table laid for tea. A big, fat woman with red hair sat before the fire and a big, fat ginger cat sat on her lap, purring. The cat had a kind face but the woman looked sour.

"No, I didn't," said the boy, whose name was Fred. "But I got something else, Ma, I got a little dorg!"

The fat woman looked so angry that Mike drew back inside Fred's coat in alarm.

"You've got the cheek to stand there and tell me you spent good money on a dog when you haven't got a job?" she exclaimed. "You'll take it straight back where it came from."

"I can't, Ma," whined Fred. "I bought it off a

13

stall. The man won't give me my money back. Oh, let me keep it, Ma. You've got Ginger. Why shouldn't I have a pet too?"

"I pay for Ginger's food," retorted the fat woman. "Who's going to buy dog meat? Tell me that."

"I don't eat meat yet," ventured Mike. The fat ginger cat chuckled.

"It's no good talking to them," he said. "They're too stupid to understand. And don't worry. She doesn't make a fuss about anything for long."

"Is – is it nice here?" ventured Mike, and the cat yawned and grinned.

"*I* get on all right," he said. "You'll have to look after yourself, mate."

Fred took Mike out of his coat and set him down on the floor by the fire. The warmth was delightful after the cold outside and Mike wagged his tiny, curling tail.

"He likes you, Ma," said Fred hopefully. "Let me keep him – eh?"

"Oh, please yourself," said the fat woman. "Only don't expect me to pay for his licence because I'm not going to, so there!"

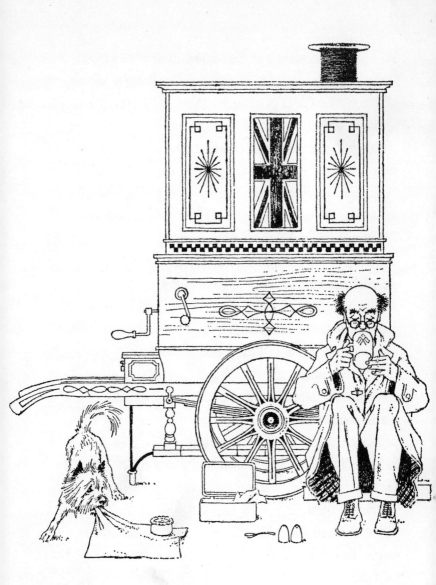

"He won't want one for ages," said Fred carelessly. "Not till he's six months old he won't. Thanks, Ma. Can I give him a drop of old Ginger's milk?"

"Hey, steady on!" exclaimed Ginger, and then, seeing Mike's hungry look, he said kindly, "oh well, I daresay I can spare you a drop. Can you lap yet?"

"Of course I can!" exclaimed Mike indignantly. "What d'you take me for? A baby?"

"Yes," said the ginger cat simply. He jumped down from the fat woman's lap and settled himself on the hearth rug by Mike's side. "I think you're a dear little chap," he said. "I don't mind dogs; so long as they behave. Let's be friends."

"I don't mind if I do," said Mike feeling suddenly much happier, and they shared the saucer of warm milk which Fred put down on the rug between them. It was the beginning of a beautiful friendship which lasted until Mike was six months old.

Living with Fred and his Ma wasn't too bad, Mike decided quite soon. True, food was always scarce, but there was the garbage in the dust bins to be explored and the food you found for yourself seemed tastier somehow than the food you got at home. Ginger didn't agree with this, but he went too when times were hard. Times were hard when Fred was out of a job. This was fairly often because he was lazy and not much good at anything, and he was always getting the sack. Then the only money that came into the house was earned by Ma, who went out cleaning, and it wasn't really enough to feed herself and Fred, let alone a dog and cat as well.

Mike did more and more food-hunting on his own and was out on the streets all day long. He grew bold and independent and learned a lot of rather naughty ways.

One evening, when Ma had come home from work and Fred was lounging about doing nothing because he was out of a job, Ma said thoughtfully:

"How old's that dog of yours now, Fred?"

"Dunno," said Fred warily. "'Bout four months?"

"Don't talk rubbish!" said Ma sharply. "It was March you brought him home. It's August now. He's over six months, and you know it."

"So what?" asked Fred uneasily.

"So he needs a licence," retorted Ma. "You want to get us into trouble with the police?"

"Lend us the seven and six, Ma?" asked Fred hopefully.

There was a long silence. Mike looked anxiously at Ma and even Ginger stopped washing behind his ears and listened to what she was going to say.

"Now, see here, Fred," said Ma. "If you want to keep a dog you've got to pay for it yourself. I work hard for my money and it's as much as I can do to feed my Ginger, let alone your Mike. If you can't find the seven and six you'd best get rid of the creature before there's trouble. Take him round to the R.S.P.C.A."

"What's that?" Mike asked Ginger uneasily. Ginger looked most uncomfortable.

"They're people who – er – who look after sick animals," he said at last.

"But I'm not sick!" said Mike. "Ginger, what's going on? Please tell me the truth. I can take it."

"Come outside," said Ginger, and the two animals slipped quietly out of the room. Ma and Fred didn't notice because they were arguing fiercely.

In the street Ginger turned and looked Mike squarely in the face.

"You'd better have it straight, chum," he said.

"The R.S.P.C.A. are kind, good people, but when a dog or cat isn't wanted any more they – they put it to sleep."

"For *good*?" whispered Mike. Ginger nodded solemnly.

"But – why?"

"Because there aren't enough owners to go around," explained Ginger sadly. "It's better than being a homeless stray."

"Is it?" demanded Mike. "Who says so?"

"Well, most people do, and I expect they're right. Dogs and cats can't look after themselves. They need owners. You see, we've been what's called domesticated animals for thousands of years. We need people, and people need us, only there aren't people enough to go around."

Mike looked about him cautiously. The street was empty, but even so he put his mouth close to Ginger's ear before he spoke.

"What happens if a dog decides to live all on his own?" he whispered breathlessly.

Ginger looked doubtful.

"He'd have to be tough," he said. "He'd have to keep out of the way of the police. Every man's hand would be against him. He'd have to find his own food."

"I do that most of the time now," said Mike bitterly.

"I know you do, but still— look Mike, wait a bit and see what happens. Perhaps Fred will buy you a licence after all and then everything will be all right."

"It won't," said Mike gloomily. "A licence only lasts for a year. I'll have this worry hanging over me for the rest of my life."

"That's true," said Ginger sadly.

" 'Tisn't as if I was really fond of Fred," Mike told him thoughtfully. "He's never been a proper master to me – training me and all that. I'd just as soon be on my own."

"Don't do anything hastily," Ginger implored him. "Stray dogs—" he broke off abruptly as the door of the house opened and Fred appeared holding a piece of string.

"Here, Mike – where are you? Good dog! Time for your walk, Mike!" he said.

"Walk, my foot!" growled Mike softly. "When has he ever taken me for a walk on a string? I know where he plans to take me and I'm not going. I'm young and strong and I can look after myself." He shrank into the shadows while Fred went on calling:

"Here, Mike! Mike! Come on then, good dog!"

"Traitor!" hissed Mike. "Good-bye, Ginger. Wish me luck. I'm off!"

Fred caught one last glimpse of the small, shaggy little figure and gave chase, but Mike had gone, scurrying through the darkening streets with wildly beating heart. He heard Fred's pounding footsteps behind him and then suddenly a soft, doggy voice whispered, "In here – quick!" A plank slid back. Mike squeezed through, and found himself on a dark wharf with the oily waters of the Thames lapping against the piles down below. The pounding footsteps went past and died away in the distance, and Mike dropped panting to the ground.

"Well!" said the strange dog quietly. "That was a narrow squeak. Are you on the run? So am I. Licence trouble? Same here. What shall we do now?"

Mike sat up. His breath came more easily and his eyes were beginning to accustom themselves to the gloom. He saw in front of him a dog, smaller than himself, with the flattened nose of a pug. Her large,

lustrous eyes were full of tears and her smooth coat
was muddy and wet.

"Do?" said Mike, suddenly feeling braver and
more cheerful now that he had a companion. "I'll
tell you what we'll do. We'll form a gang and I'll be
the leader. What's your name? Tizzy? Well, Tizzy,
this looks a good spot for a hideout. We can sleep in
those barrels there and come and go by the loose
board. By day we'll look for food and by night
we'll hunt rats for sport and tell yarns, and lead a
wild, carefree life! We'll find other dogs to join us,
chaps without a home and a master!"

"Oh Mike!" breathed Tizzy. "That'll be mar-
vellous! I was so scared, and now you've come
along, so strong and brave, just to look after little
me."

Mike swaggered to the middle of the wharf and
jumped onto a big packing case left there by the
men who had been unloading a barge. He drew
himself up to his full height, his ears erect and his
tail proudly curved over his back. Behind him the
dark river flowed silently, the reflection from street
lamps wriggling sinuously in the ripples like golden
snakes. From the distance came the low growl of

traffic, but on the wharf itself silence wrapped the two little dogs around.

"I am Mike!" said the small dog on the packing case. "I am an outcast with every man's hand against me, but my life is my own and no one shall take it from me. I don't believe dogs really need owners. From now on I shall be the leader of a lawless gang and this wharf shall be our hideout and our home!"

2 : Tizzy

For a few moments after Mike stopped speaking there was silence on the old wharf. Far down below the water lapped softly, and a few bits of old newspaper rustled in the light summer breeze. Then Tizzy sighed, a long, low, mournful sigh.

"What's up?" asked Mike, jumping down from the box. "Don't you like the sound of it? Cheer up, Tiz, we'll have a wonderful time!"

"Yes, I expect we will," said Tizzy, with an effort at cheerfulness. "Yes, of course we will."

"Oy!" said Mike. "Snap out of it, baby! You're depressed?"

"Oh, it's nothing – only—"

"Only what?"

"Only I wish I was sure you're right about dogs not needing owners."

"Oh, that," said Mike carelessly. "Of course I'm right. What good are they, anyway?"

"They give you a home," said Tizzy wistfully.

"Only as long as it suits them," Mike told her.

"When it comes to finding seven and six they chuck you out."

"Not all of them, surely," said Tizzy. "Perhaps we've just been unlucky."

"Us and about five thousand others!" said Mike. "I met a chap once who'd been in a Dogs' Home, and he knew what he was talking about, he did. He'd talked to lots of other dogs and heard their stories, and he said he wouldn't give you tuppence for an owner. Better off on your own, he said, if you've got any sense at all, he said. And that's what I think, too. You take my owner, Fred. Bought me for five bob, he did, just because his mother had a cat and he didn't see why he shouldn't keep a pet too. Then, when he'd got me he didn't really want me. He never trained me, or bothered with me at all, and when he realized I was six months old he—" Mike paused and stared angrily out across the dark river. "He was going to have me – you know."

"Um," said Tizzy. "I know. All the same I still think that a *good* owner would be nicer than being on one's own."

"All right then," said Mike huffily. "You don't

have to join my gang. Go and find yourself a good owner."

"Don't be mean," said Tizzy. "You know I can't."

"Yes you can. You can go and sit on the edge of the pavement looking sad, and presently someone will come along and say, 'Oh look at that poor little dog! I believe she's lost.' And they'll take you home."

Tizzy gave a short laugh. "You're joking, of course," she said. "What they'd do is they'd take me to the police and say, 'Here's a stray dog,' and the police would take me to the Dogs' Home and then, if they couldn't find anyone to buy me they'd – er – they'd—"

"You're right," said Mike. "So you see, you're much better off in my gang."

"It's the Pedigree People who get all the good homes," Tizzy said resentfully. "All those snobs who are born in grand kennels and get their pictures in the newspapers for winning prizes at shows. They make me sick."

Mike didn't reply. He was watching a rat hole in the side of one of the black sheds which stood on the wharf. A lean, hairy face with whiskers was peeping out. Mike pounced, and hit his nose hard against the shed. The rat, safe inside its hole, giggled.

"Clumsy!" he said.

"All right, my friend. I'll get you one day," growled Mike rubbing his nose ruefully with a paw.

"You didn't want to *eat* it, did you?" asked Tizzy distastefully.

"No, of course not. I just don't like rats. All the same, I could do with a bite to eat right now. How about you, Tiz?"

"I could nibble a little something," admitted Tizzy.

"Let's go garbaging then," suggested Mike. "I'll tell you something interesting, Tiz. In America they call dust bins garbage cans, or trash cans."

"How do you know?" asked Tizzy unbelievingly.

"Because as it happens, I just happen to know a chap from America," said Mike triumphantly. "He says he's a Boston bull terrier and he came over here with his owner and spent six months shut up in quarantine and when at last he came out he had to go and get lost."

"How?" asked Tizzy.

"I forget. He did tell me. Anyway, he got lost and he liked being on his own so much that he just stayed lost. Seems his owner was terribly rich and lived in hotels and this chap simply hated it. We used to go out together a lot, and he taught me heaps of American words. He used to say 'C'm on, buddy, let's go have ourselves a good trash can!'" Mike sighed. "I wish I could find him again. He'd be a splendid person for my gang. He was really tough. You'd never have thought he was a Pedigree Person."

"He sounds silly to me," said Tiz jealously.

"He wasn't silly; he was great. I tell you what, Tiz, let's go and have a look in the bins behind the Hilton Hotel. We might meet Boston Bill (that's what I called him) there. There's always a lot of American food in those bins and he fancied a bit of home cooking, Bill did. I could just do with a leg of fried chicken myself! Come on."

"Where is this Hilton Hotel?" asked Tizzy. "Is it far? I'm tired."

Mike looked at her shrewdly. He knew well enough that Tizzy was jealous, and he also knew that if ever he was to form a gang it would just have to stop. One jealous person in a gang would be enough to wreck the whole thing.

"Tiz," he said, "listen to me."

"I'm listening," said Tiz sulkily.

"Do you want to join my gang or don't you?"

"You haven't got a gang yet."

"No, but I will have, and when I do I shall treat everyone the same. No special treatment. So if you don't want to be a good gang member, friends with everyone and no jealousy, now's the time to say so. You can go off on your own and no harm done. What do you say?"

"I found this wharf first," said Tizzy, and sniffed loudly.

"All right, so it's your wharf. Me and my gang will find a hideout somewhere else. Want me to go?"

"*No!*" burst out Tiz, beginning to cry in earnest. "No, Mike, don't leave me, please! I'm sorry I was silly about Boston Bill. If we meet him I'll be nice to him, I promise. Only don't l-leave me, Mike. I'm a poor little dog with no owner—"

"Oh, phooey!" said Mike. "Come on then. Follow me. Hilton trash cans, here we come!"

It was now very late, but as the two dogs made

their way into the heart of London, the streets were still brightly lit and full of cars taking people home from theatres, or to restaurants for supper. The night was warm and the air balmy and it went to Mike's head like wine.

"Whoopee!" he shouted, scampering up Whitehall and into Trafalgar Square. "This is the life! Look at all those pigeons, Tiz – think you could catch one?"

"I might if they came down here," giggled Tizzy, craning her short, thick neck to see the pigeons roosting on roofs and ledges high up in the air. Then she gave a violent start, bumped into Mike and exclaimed:

"Lions!"

"Where?" asked Mike.

"There! Look, four of them! Huge, enormous lions! Oh, Mike, let's get out of here!"

"Don't be a dope," said Mike calmly. "They aren't real, they're made of stone."

"Are – are you sure?" quavered Tizzy.

"Of course I'm sure," scoffed Mike. He swaggered up to the base of Nelson's Column, which is guarded by the big stone lions at each corner,

climbed the steps and sniffed casually at the nearest lion's face. Then he sat down, stretched a little wearily and called:

"Let's have a rest, Tiz. Come and sit here by me."

Tiz followed him up the steps and sat down beside him. "It's nice here," she said.

"Jolly nice," said Mike. "We're seeing life, that's what. Keep a lookout for policemen, though."

The two little dogs leaned back comfortably against Nelson's Column and looked at the lights and the people and the cars and the big red buses. At last Mike said:

"You haven't told me yet how you came to run off, Tiz."

"No more I have," said Tizzy. "I don't suppose it's anything like as exciting as your adventures, Mike. As a matter of fact it's a bit sad, not exciting at all."

"Sorry to hear that," said Mike gruffly. "Don't cry, old girl."

"I'm all right," said Tiz. She scratched her right ear while she struggled to control herself. "Just a moment's weakness. Better now. Well, what happened was this; my owners moved away and they – they left me behind."

"Never!" exclaimed Mike.

"They did. You see, my licence was due for renewal, because I'm one and a half now. They bought the first one all right, but when the time came around again, everything had gone wrong. They had to move because their house was going to be pulled down, and at the new place they were going to – a flat, it was – they weren't allowed to keep a dog. So what with one thing and another they – they just left me behind."

"But that's awful!"

"I know," said Tizzy sadly. "It was such a shock to me. I'd heard them talking about it, you see, but I never really believed they'd just go off and leave me. They'd always been quite decent to me in their own way. I liked *her* very much, although I wasn't so keen on *him*. Well, on the day they moved I just popped out to say good-bye to my friends and when I came back they'd gone!"

"So what did you do?" inquired Mike curiously.

"I cried," admitted Tizzy. "I just howled, until the people next door threw an old boot at me. It hurt, so I started off to try and find where my people had gone, but of course it was hopeless. I ran around the streets until I was worn out. Then I found that loose board in the fence and I went on to the wharf and slept in a barrel. The next day I searched again, but I had no luck, and I was just going back to the wharf to sleep when you came along."

"They might have tried to find you another home!" said Mike hotly. "I told you owners were no good, Tiz. Surely you must agree that I'm right?"

"A good owner would be lovely," said Tizzy longingly. "A dear, good owner who really loved one and wouldn't dream of going away and leaving their little dog; an owner who always had the seven and sixpence—"

"I suppose you believe in fairies too?" asked Mike sarcastically. "There aren't any owners like that, Tiz. Anyway, I've never met one and neither have you."

"Perhaps it's because we're not Pedigree People," ventured Tizzy, but Mike shook his head.

"Doesn't make any difference. Look at my pal, Boston Bill. He's as Pedigree as they come and his owner was rolling in money, but was she a good owner? No. She had him shut up in quarantine kennels for months and months and, when he came out, he had to live in a huge great hotel and never go out except in the car, or on a leash. A page boy took him walking and he *never* let him off. Bill told me he nearly went mad. Then at last he did escape – I forget how – and now he's really happy. Which reminds me, we must push on. The Hilton Hotel is miles from here, and I'm so hungry I could almost eat *you*!"

Tizzy gave a girlish giggle. "Catch me if you can!" she called, and darted across Trafalgar Square towards Lower Regent Street.

Somewhere, not very far away, a clock struck twelve.

"Big Ben," said Mike. "Golly, it's late. We'd better hurry or the cats will have had all the best bits."

"I hate cats," panted Tizzy, hurrying along at his side. "I'd kill cats if I got half a chance."

"Oh, they're not all bad," said Mike tolerantly. "There was a pretty good cat where I used to live. Ginger, his name was. We were pals. Good old Ginger; I'd like to see him again but I don't suppose I ever shall." He sighed. "It's a sad, sad life, full of partings. Turn right here, Tiz, now at the next corner I think we'll find – yes, it is, the Hilton. Now, did you ever see a better lot of garbage cans?"

Tizzy sniffed the air. "I smell something good," she said and trotted over to the nearest bin. The lid shot up and an angry cat face looked out.

"Buzz off!" said the cat furiously. The lid dropped down again, and from inside the bin came the sound of somebody crunching fish bones.

"No manners," said Tizzy bitterly. "I told you I hated cats."

"Never mind. There are enough bins for all," said Mike soothingly. "Who wants fish, anyway? Only fit for cats. Now, I can smell steak!"

"What – in a dust bin?" exclaimed Tizzy and Mike said, "Sure. The people in these big hotels are so rich they don't bother to clean up their plates. 'I've had enough steak,' they say. 'Chuck it in the trash can!' they say."

"*Honestly?*" asked Tizzy, her eyes very round.

"Cross my heart," Mike told her solemnly.

"That's right, honey," said a strange voice. Tizzy

37

jumped violently as from behind the biggest bin emerged a dog with a face not so very different from her own.

"Boston Bill!" exclaimed Mike happily. "The very chap we hoped to see!"

3 : Boston Bill

"How dy'do, folks?" said Bill, grinning all over his face. "Who's the little lady, Mike? Introduce me, please."

"Tizzy – Boston Bill. Boston Bill – Tizzy," said Mike rapidly. "It's good to see you again, old sport."

"Long time no see," replied Bill. He beamed at Tizzy, good nature in every fold of his wrinkled muzzle. "It's a great pleasure to meet you, my dear. I had no idea, when I stopped by for a little supper, that I should have such charming company. Let me recommend the third can from the left. The garbage in that one comes straight from the private suites, and boy! do those folks feed themselves well!"

"You seem to know a lot about it," said Mike, and Bill smiled.

"I do, brother, I do. I lived in this little old hotel myself for months, and in a private suite at that. We lived it up all right. Caviar! *Paté de fois gras!* Marrow bones! Sole *à la bonne femme*!"

"What on earth's that?" asked Tizzy.

"Fish. Just plain old fish, but mussed up a bit, you know. As far as I'm concerned the cats can have it. Give me good red meat! Rare beef, that's for me."

"Me too," said Mike. "Let's turn the can over, Bill. Then we can sort it out."

"Won't it make an awful noise?" asked Tizzy nervously. "Won't someone hear us and come out and – and throw things?"

Boston Bill grinned. "Sister, you haven't lived," he said kindly. "Mean to tell me you don't know how to sort the contents of a trash can?"

"No, I'm afraid I don't," said Tizzy apologetically. "You see, in my last home they never let me out at night."

"Too bad," said Bill. "Well, it's simple really. All you need is the know-how. Ready, Mike?"

Mike nodded, and trotted behind the bin. Gently he began to push, while Boston Bill used his weight to steady the tall bin on the other side. Slowly it tipped, and gently slid to the ground. The lid rolled off with a clang and the three dogs held their breath.

"You're losing your touch," whispered Bill reprovingly. "You should have caught that lid."

"Trust dogs to make a row!" snarled a furious cat voice from farther along the line. "Spoiling everything for other people!"

"Shut up or I'll bite you!" snarled Tizzy, showing all her teeth.

"Steady!" said Bill. "Live and let live, honey. We're in the wrong this time. Still, no harm done," he added as the quiet of the dark street was unbroken by the sound of any human voice. "Let's get to work. Mike, it's your go."

Mike disappeared inside the tall bin and the other two heard the sound of scrabbling. Then out shot a stream of garbage and presently Mike emerged, flushed and triumphant, with custard clinging to his whiskers.

"It's a bonanza tonight!" he whispered. "There's the best part of a cake down at the bottom. Got a sweet tooth, Tiz?"

Tizzy did not answer. She had already picked out a chicken leg and was happily gnawing it in the gutter.

"Steak – lamb chop – veal cutlet," said Bill

thoughtfully. "Boy, oh boy, do they look good! And to think that when I lived in that hotel I never had any appetite. The waiter brought up my meals in a beautiful china dish, the meat cut up small and mixed with brown bread and vegetables, for my health." He gave a short laugh. "Health? I always felt sick, I can tell you that. But now – feel my muscle, Tizzy, just feel."

"Can't," muttered Tizzy with her mouth full. "Later."

"There's half a roast pheasant here," said Mike. "Do you fancy it, old chap, or may I—?"

"Go ahead," said Bill. "Finders keepers. I'll make out with these ribs of beef."

There was a long, contented silence only broken by the sound of gnawing and chewing and the crunching of bones. At last, when the three dogs could eat no more, Mike sighed, stretched and said:

"Well, what now? Bill, would you care to come back with us for the night? We can offer you a shakedown in a barrel, and there's something I'd like to discuss with you after we've had some sleep."

"Sure, sure," said Boston Bill, licking the grease

carefully off his paws. "Now then, you cats, you can move in and clear up after we leave."

"Thanks for nothing," snarled the angry cat who had spoken before. "You didn't leave anything worth having. Dogs! Why can't you stay with your owners, eh?"

"Why should we?" demanded Mike. "You don't."

"That's different," said the cat. "We don't care if we have owners or not. Sometimes we choose to live with humans, but they don't own us, *we* own *them*."

"You're a lot of swell heads," chipped in Boston Bill. "You think you own the earth."

"So we do," retorted the cat. "We're free and independent. We come and go as we wish. Even if we choose to live in a house someone always leaves a window open for us to come and go. Can you dogs say the same?"

"You've got a point there," admitted Bill. "Nevertheless—"

"Oh, don't argue with him," implored Mike. "You can't win. Cats always have answers to everything."

"I hate them," said Tizzy angrily and she made a run at the cat, who arched his back and hissed like a snake.

"Want to make something out of it?" he asked dangerously. Tizzy faltered and fell back. From in and around the other bins more cat faces appeared, grinning at her discomfiture.

"Come on," said Mike hastily. "We've got to go."

It was such a hot night that all three slept outside, stretched on the still-warm stones of the wharf. Mike awakened first, just as the sun came up, and he roused the other two playfully by rolling them over on to their backs and pretending to bite them in their middles.

"Cut it out," said Boston Bill sleepily. "I'm too old for fun and games before breakfast. Well, what do we do now?"

"We clear out of here before the workmen arrive," Mike told him. "Let's go down and lie by the water. I want to talk."

Not far from the wharf, on the edge of the river, there was a little pebbly beach. It was rather dirty and smelly, but the dogs didn't notice that. They

44

stretched out lazily, hidden from anyone above by a jutting piece of wall, and they hardly moved even when a wave, made by a passing motor launch, swept up the beach and licked at their feet.

"Jolly here," said Mike contentedly. "Just like the seaside, I'll bet."

"Brother!" said Boston Bill. "It's about as much like the seaside as you're like a pedigree cairn. I don't want to seem snide," he added hastily.

"That's all right," replied Mike. "Have you been to the seaside, Bill?"

"Have I been—! I'll say I have. South of France, Italian Riviera, Honolulu, Long Island—"

"I once knew a dog who went to Brighton," cut in Tizzy. "Her owners took her for the day."

"I've always heard Brighton is swell," said Bill politely. "But what was it you wanted to talk to me about, Mike, my friend?"

Mike hesitated. He had begun to feel shy about asking Boston Bill to join his gang. Bill was so grand, and so widely travelled, and he was so much older than either Tizzy or himself. Probably Bill would consider joining a gang a kid's game. Or if he did join he might want to be the boss, and Mike wouldn't like that at all.

But then he looked at Bill's friendly, honest, wrinkled face, at the broad, manly chest and the alert prick ears and he knew he desperately wanted to be with Bill, who was brave and straight, without an ounce of meanness in him. If being a Pedigree Person made you as nice as Bill, perhaps it wasn't such a bad thing after all.

He took a deep breath.

"I'm forming a gang," he said. "A gang of dogs who haven't any owners. We'll be outside the law so we'll have to be constantly on the lookout for danger from policemen and people from the Dogs' Home. We'll have to find our own food and shelter and – well – look after ourselves."

"I've been doing that for a long time now," said Boston Bill thoughtfully.

"And have you enjoyed it?" inquired Tizzy anxiously.

"Well, yes and no. I've been a lot happier than when I was living in swell hotels and going into quarantine every time my owner decided to live in Europe for a while. But I'm not going to say I wouldn't rather have a *good* owner than none at all."

"There aren't any good owners," growled Mike.

"Oh come now, I wouldn't say that. Few and far between perhaps, but they do exist. I recall a pekingese I knew once in good ole New York. She belonged to an owner I'd have given my eye teeth for. A beautiful friendship theirs was – beautiful."

"I expect the pekingese was a Pedigree Person," said Tizzy resentfully.

"Well yes, she was. But really that doesn't make any difference."

"That's what you think," said Mike gloomily. "Me and Tizzy know different. So you want to find another owner, Bill?"

"Now, I didn't say that," protested Bill. "What's your proposition, Mike? You want me to join your gang?"

"I'd be jolly pleased," said Mike. He hesitated a moment and went on, "You can be the leader if you like."

"No, no!" protested Bill. "It's your gang. If I join I join as an ordinary member." He scratched one ear thoughtfully, grunting a little as he did so.

Then he nibbled a hind leg, got up, gave himself a shake and sat down again.

"That's better," he said. "I feel a little neater now. I'd like time to think about the gang idea if you don't mind, Mike. I never rush into things."

"Take your time," said Mike. He felt a little disappointed that Bill hadn't jumped at the idea of joining the gang. It was such a splendid idea and they would have such fine times. Oh well—

"Tell us how you escaped from your owner," he said. "Tiz would like to know, wouldn't you, Tiz?"

"Very much," said Tiz politely. She admired Boston Bill for his good looks and his man-of-the-world air, but she still, she told herself, liked Mike best. Mike was her sort, after all.

"There's not much to it," said Bill modestly. "I just used my brains, that's all. The trouble was I never went out alone – never. Always with my owner or her husband or her secretary or her chauffeur or her maid or one of the page boys from whichever hotel we happened to be staying in at the time. You see, I happen to be extremely valuable. Please don't think I'm boasting. Money means nothing to me. I only tell you this so that you'll understand why I was always under guard. I'd be a rich prize for a dog thief."

"Golly!" said Tiz.

"How much are you worth?" asked Mike curiously.

"My owner paid a thousand dollars for me when I was only six months old," said Boston Bill. "Both my parents and all my grandparents were full champions in the States. My, my! They were a classy bunch!"

"They must have been," said Mike respectfully. "You still haven't told us how you got away."

"It was simple, but clever," chuckled Bill. "I practised blowing myself up."

"*What?*" exclaimed both the other dogs in chorus, and Mike added, "With dynamite?"

"No, of course not. Blowing myself up like a bullfrog. I tensed all the muscles in my neck and took a deep breath and held it, so that when they put my collar on –" he paused to laugh heartily – "they buckled it in the last hole. I remember how the secretary and the maid agreed I seemed to be getting fat! After that, of course, it was easy to escape."

He stopped talking and stretched himself out on his side. "Delightful down here by the water," he murmured. "Think I'll catch forty winks."

Mike and Tizzy looked at each other. Mike raised his eyebrows questioningly and Tiz shook her head.

"We don't understand," said Mike hesitantly. "How did puffing yourself up help you to escape?"

"Elementary, my dear fellow," said Bill sleepily. "When we got out into the park I just slipped the loose collar over my head and off I went. Most successful plots are quite simple, you know. They never saw me again, although I imagine they offered the most enormous reward. I lay very low, I can tell you, until I was sure they'd all gone back to the States."

"How did you know?" asked Tizzy curiously. Bill chuckled again.

"I was watching around the corner when they drove off to the airport," he said. "I'd been living in a very snug little cellar quite close to the hotel all the time. That was six months ago, and I've been left in peace ever since. It's been great." He rose and stretched, first his front legs, then his back. "Let's go and find something to eat," he said. "Oh, and by the way, Mike, I've thought the matter over and I'll be happy to join your gang."

4 : Shep

Mike, Tizzy and Boston Bill had a very pleasant little lunch of sausages eaten while lying low among some bushes in Hyde Park. Mike had stolen the sausages from a butcher's shop. It was wrong of him but he did not know any better and believed himself to be very clever. The butcher had not noticed until much too late, and Mike laughed as told the other two – who were waiting just down the street – how he had sneaked in behind a customer pretending to be her dog, and then, when the butcher turned away to cut off some chops, how he had made a flying leap, yanked the sausages off the hook and vanished at the speed of light.

Tizzy made rather a pig of herself over the sausages. She had never tasted them before. Boston Bill thought them as good as the sausages he had eaten in France and Italy and Mike just ate silently, one eye watching for policemen, as always.

When the sausages were all gone they felt thirsty, and Mike led the way across the park and into

Kensington Gardens, where they drank from the Round Pond. A few children were sailing boats, but not many because it was midday and the ones who were well brought up had gone home to lunch. The children who were left came from homes where mothers go out to work, leaving the kids some money to buy potato chips and ice-cream. These children sat around the pond, bare feet dangling in the cool water, munching chips and throwing greasy bits of newspaper on the grass.

"Messy," said Bill disapprovingly. "Why, even a dog knows what a litter bin is for."

One of the boys tried to entice Mike into the water by throwing in sticks for him, but Mike, although greatly tempted, refused.

"For one thing I'm too full of sausage," he said reluctantly, looking longingly at the nice, cool water. "And for another I'm not going to push my luck. We've kept clear of park keepers so far, but if I go swimming I bet they'd soon be buzzing around us like bees. Come on you two, let's clear out. I don't trust little boys, they've got some very nasty ways."

"You don't trust anybody," said Tizzy a little

disapprovingly, and Mike grunted, "You're right I don't. And that's going to be one of the rules of my gang, Tiz. Trust nobody."

"It's rather horrid," said Tiz. "Don't we even trust each other?"

"Of course we do!" exclaimed Mike. "I was talking about humans. Naturally one can trust dogs."

"What about cats?"

"Hm. Hard to say. Some are all right, and some aren't. You'll have to use your own judgment about cats," said Mike.

"Never trust a Siamese," put in Bill. "They're up to every trick in the book."

"What are Siamese?" asked Tizzy, her round eyes very wide.

"Foreigners," said Mike shortly. "Petted, pampered foreigners with shocking voices. We're not likely to meet any down our way." He paused, and went on, "Hullo-ullo-ullo – what's going on here?"

By now the dogs had left Kensington Gardens and were back in the wide open spaces of Hyde Park. On one side of them lay Rotten Row, where a few horseback riders were trotting up and down. On the other side was a roped in enclosure with quite a crowd of people standing around. It was impossible to see what was going on, but from the enclosure came the baa-ing of sheep.

"What gives?" asked Bill.

"Oh, do let's go and see!" begged Tizzy excitedly.

"Better find out first what it is," advised Mike. He stopped a small white dog who was following his owner across the grass and said:

"Pardon me, but do you know what's up, over there?"

The white dog looked at him contemptuously.

"Sheep dog trials," he said. "Everybody knows that."

"Snob!" said Mike bitterly. "Sheep dog trials? What on earth's that?"

"Your guess is as good as mine," said Boston Bill. "Let's go and take a look."

Carefully, worming their way through the forest of legs, the three dogs made their way to the edge of the roped off enclosure. What they saw there amazed them. A small bunch of sheep were being guided by a large dog very, very slowly and carefully, along a course marked out by flags. Every now and then a sheep would try to break away and then the dog would skim silently over the grass and the sheep went meekly back into its place. Standing on one side of the course, a man in rough country clothes guided the dog by whistling to him. Whistle! and the dog dropped to the ground. Whistle! He was up and driving the sheep gently on. Whistle! Now he was coaxing the sheep through a narrow gap into a corral made of willow. Whistle! He dropped again and guarded the gap. Everybody began to clap and the man in rough clothes looked pleased.

"Two minutes, forty-five seconds!" a voice called loudly, and everyone clapped again.

"This is very odd," said Mike, puzzled. "What do you make of it, Bill?"

"Must be some sort of a contest," drawled Bill. "That fellow over there, the sheep dog, has to get his sheep around the course and home quicker than anyone else. Skilled work, I'd say."

"Isn't he *handsome*?" breathed Tizzy. Mike looked at her sourly.

"Bit of a country bumpkin, if you ask me," he growled. "Look, there's another one just going to begin."

Four more sheep had appeared in the charge of a new dog, a large, silky coated collie with a long, pointed nose. He looked extremely nervous and kept licking his lips and casting anxious glances at his master, who scowled at him and muttered something under his breath.

"Now there's a man I wouldn't be owned by, not for all the tea in China!" exclaimed Mike.

"They're off!" said Bill. "That poor fellow is a bundle of nerves. I'll bet that man beats him if he doesn't win."

Whistle! The big collie started off, edging the sheep cautiously between the flags. The sheep seemed to sense his nervousness, for they were restless and kept breaking away. The collie's ears began to fly wildly as he raced around, trying to keep the sheep in a close bunch. The angry man whistled shrilly and waved his arm. The dog hesitated, clearly puzzled and uncertain what he should do. People began to laugh, and that was the last straw for the already nervous sheep. Suddenly they broke away, charging through the crowd. They scattered far and wide and then stopped, nibbling at the grass and looking nervously over their shoulders for the dog.

But the collie, after one horrified glance at his master, had disappeared completely!

"Brother! There's big trouble coming to that guy," said Bill sympathetically.

"It wasn't his fault!" cried Tizzy. "That beastly man said something which made him nervous."

"Owners!" said Mike in disgust. "They're all tarred with the same brush. I'll tell you what, let's go after that poor chap and see what we can do to help."

"Oh yes, do let's!" cried Tizzy. "He's ever so handsome – in a country sort of way," she added hastily as Bill shot her an amused glance. "He's not as handsome as you are, Bill dear."

"Which way did he go?" asked Mike.

"Way over there," said Bill. "He's making for Piccadilly, and if he gets caught in traffic he's really in trouble. He's only a country hick. After him, folks, as fast as you can make it."

Mike glanced around the crowd. The man, very red in the face and angry, was pushing his way out of the circle of people, whistling and calling to the dog, but everyone else seemed to have forgotten about him, and already a new bunch of sheep were being herded carefully along the course by a bob-tailed sheep dog from the Sussex Downs.

Mike took to his heels, the other two following close behind.

They caught up with the frightened collie just as he reached the gates at Hyde Park Corner. He was hesitating, in a pitiful state of terror, while the traffic whirled by in a never ending stream and his master's angry voice came faintly from behind. Advancing toward him, with slow, majestic tread, was a large London policeman. In fact, danger threatened from all sides.

Mike summed up the situation in a flash. Bumping into the collie's flank he whispered urgently:

"We're friends! Follow me if you wish to be saved!"

The collie gave him a startled look, but he did as he was told, and the next second all four dogs were safely hidden in a clump of bushes just inside the park railings. On one side of them feet clattered on the pavement and huge scarlet buses growled and grunted on their way to Piccadilly Circus, while on the other side, hooves thundered as the riders in the Row galloped by, but in the bushes there was sanctuary and the four breathless dogs lay down and panted, tongues lolling out.

"That was a close shave," said Boston Bill at last, looking kindly at the dejected figure of the collie.

"Well, you *are* in trouble," said Mike. "What's your name, eh?"

"Shep," said the collie. "I be real grateful to you gentlemen for your help." He spoke with a broad West Country accent which made Tizzy giggle. "And to the lady too," Shep went on, glancing shyly at Tizzy's little flat face, so unlike his own.

"Think nothing of it," grunted Mike. "We'd been watching, and it struck us you weren't getting a square deal from that owner of yours. He got you muddled up with his signals in some way, didn't he?"

"I didn't rightly understand him," said Shep looking bewildered. "Maybe I was to blame, but them signals he gave me wasn't what we'd agreed on down home-along. Reckon he got a bit flustered like, with the crowd an' all. And them sheep just lost their heads, like sheep always do. Oh deary me, there'll be a terrible to-do about all this when we gets home. He'll take it out of me proper, he will."

"What will he do?" inquired Tizzy fearfully. "Will he – beat you?"

The collie gave a short, unhappy laugh.

" 'Twouldn't be the first time," he said briefly. "Well, reckon I'd better be getting on back. The longer I stays away the worse it'll be. I never ought to have run off, but when all them people started to laugh I lost my nerve; went all to pieces I did. Hardly knew what I was doing."

"Wait a minute," said Mike. "Why go back at all?"

The collie sat bolt upright in surprise and his fringed ears stood straight out from his head, as his deep, golden eyes grew round.

"Not go back?" he stammered. "Not go back? But – I've got my job to do!"

"Do you like doing it?" demanded Bill.

"No. No, I don't. 'Tis terrible hard, and I suffer from my nerves when I have to go in for these trials. But – not go back! Why, what else is there for me to do? Dogs must have owners. I may only be a country lad from Devonshire and not so smart as you, but I do know that."

"Have you got a licence?" inquired Tizzy. Shep shook his head.

"Don't need one," he told her. "Working dogs is exempt."

"Oh, well then," said Mike. "What do you want with an owner? So far as I can see the only, and mark my words, Shep, I say *only*, use for owners is to buy you a licence so you don't get heart failure every time you see a policeman. Why go back to that man at all? Come and join my gang and be free as the air! No more competitions, no more nerves, no more tiresome sheep! Just good comradeship and adventure and fun!"

"A gang?" said Shep slowly. "What be that then?"

"It's a band of brothers," said Bill.

"And sisters," put in Tizzy jealously.

"A band of good comrades," said Mike. "All for one and one for all. We've got a hideout on an old wharf where we sleep, and we go out after dark and raid dust bins and have the most *super* meals."

"Fried chicken," put in Tizzy, licking her lips. Shep looked terribly shocked.

"Killing chickens is a crime," he said fearfully. "You gets shot for killing chickens."

"Not in London you don't," Mike assured him. "They're dead already."

"Oh deary me!" groaned Shep. "Lunnon sounds a terrible lawless place. What else do you eat?"

"Lamb chops!" said Bill. "Yum Yum!"

Shep fairly shot to his feet, his face wrinkled up in dismay.

"Sheep killing be the worst of all!" he gasped.

"Oh, sit down!" Mike implored him. "You've got it all wrong, old chap. None of us kill anything. I give you my word. Look – come back with us to our hideout and we'll explain everything. O.K.?"

Shep thought hard. They could see how troubled he was and they pitied him deeply, but he had to make up his own mind. At last he slowly shook his head.

"I'll have to go back," he said sadly. "I feels it to be my duty."

"You're a chump," grunted Mike disgustedly but Boston Bill said kindly:

"He must do what his conscience tells him, Mike. All right, if that's how you feel we'll walk over with you and bid you good-bye. I hope your master won't be too hard on you, old pal."

"He will," said Shep gloomily. "But there it be."

The four dogs had been in the bushes for some time, and already the shadows were growing longer and the nurse-maids and the young mothers were taking their children home to supper and bed. As the dogs trotted soberly over the grass, Mike noticed that the crowds were less thick and the sounds of baa-ing no longer floated on the breeze. Hope rose in his breast and he pressed forward eagerly towards the roped in enclosure where the sheep dog trials had been held.

All was gone – the ropes, the crowds, the poles, the flags, the sheep, the men and the dogs! The judge's table had been cleared away and even the tent where people had been drinking beer. There was nothing left at all except an old, old man collecting bits of waste paper on the end of a pointed stick.

Mike turned triumphantly and confronted Shep

who was staring in utter bewilderment at the empty scene.

"You see!" said Mike. "Your precious owner has abandoned you and gone home. Now will you join my gang?"

"Oh, do!" cried Tizzy, and Bill said, "You'd be welcome, buddy, on our ole wharf."

Shep seemed too upset to speak, but he looked round at the three of them with moist, grateful eyes. Then, with hanging head and drooping tail he trotted away at their side.

5 : The Twins

The next few days were spent very pleasantly in showing Shep the sights of London. At first he was nervous, terrified of meeting his master at every corner, but the other dogs managed at last to make him understand that London was not like the little town in Devonshire which was all he had known until then.

" 'Twasn't all that small," he protested. "Over two thousand people there are in our town. Proper crowded it is on market day."

"Two thousand!" grinned Mike. "Do you know how many people live in London, Shep? More than eight *million*! Bit of a difference – eh?"

"Never!" said Shep. "You're pulling my leg, Mike. There aren't that many people in the whole world!"

"You're dead ignorant," Mike told him kindly, and he took him to Trafalgar Square during the rush hour when all the offices are closing for the day, and thousands upon thousands of people are hurrying to the big stations to make their way home. Shep watched in utter bewilderment, but it seemed to convince him that it was very unlikely that he would ever be found by his master again, and after that he settled down happily to being a member of the gang. He kept the three town dogs in fits of laughter because of his ignorance of anything outside the life on the farm, but he was such a modest, simple, good-hearted fellow that he was never offended; in fact when he realized how much he amused them, he pretended to be more of a country bumpkin than he really was. He talked in a broad Devonshire dialect which they couldn't understand, and Mike answered him in rhyming Cockney slang. Boston Bill and Tizzy agreed that it was as good as a play, and that they ought to go on television.

All in all, life on the old wharf became very pleasant indeed. The weather continued to be warm and sunny, there was plenty of food to be had and nobody bothered them. Whenever they felt in the mood for a little sport, the river rats were only too happy to oblige.

The rats lived in holes among the old stone walls

of the wharf, and their secret passages enabled them to pop up in the most unexpected places.

"Cuckoo! Can't catch me!" a large rat would suddenly chant aggravatingly from a spot just behind where the dogs were sitting. But when they wheeled around they saw nothing but the end of a long, thin tail, or a twitching whisker and from the depths of the secret passage came a mocking laugh. Tizzy, who really hated rats, sat for hours by a hole, very quiet and still like a cat, convinced that patience paid off in the end, but she never caught one, and it made the rats giggle like anything to see her sitting there, eyes glued on the hole, while they slyly crept up behind her and stole the nice bone which she had been saving up.

Mike's approach was bolder. He waited until a rat was crossing the wharf, right out in the open, and then pounced, but the rats were always too quick for him. Once he pounced so violently that he went right off the edge of the wharf into the water and had to swim ashore, coughing and spluttering, while the rats rolled around, weak with laughter.

Boston Bill really had most success. He didn't

hunt, saying he was too old for that sort of thing but he drove the rats nearly mad with rage by constantly telling the other dogs in a loud, clear voice how very small these Thames rats seemed after the American ones.

"In good ole New York the rats are more the size of cats," he would say, winking wickedly at Tizzy and Mike. "Huge, they are, and savage, not like these poor little creatures."

"We're *not* little!" the rats shouted in furious voices from all the holes on the wharf, and Bill cocked his head on one side and said, "Hark! I think I heard a mouse squeak!" Then he would egg on Shep to tell tall stories about the enormous rats the farm terriers killed down in Devonshire at threshing time.

It was all great fun, and Mike was happier than he had ever been in his life before, but one thing bothered him. He felt that four dogs did not make a gang. Four was a nice number for a little group of friends, but Mike had ambitions.

"What I want is a few tough guys," he told himself. "Tizzy is only a girl, Bill is not as young as he was, and Shep is a dear old softy. To hear him going on about lambs you'd think he was a nurse-maid, not a member of a gang. What I want is three or four chaps who really know their way around; chaps like me – bold, ruthless enemies of society!"

As this was what Mike wanted, it was really bad luck for him that the next people to join the gang should have been – the twins.

It was Shep who discovered the twins. He had gone down to the little pebbly beach late one evening to have a drink and cool his feet, sore from walking on unaccustomed city pavements, when he saw a sack come floating by. The sack was tied up at the mouth with a piece of string and must have been thrown into the water very recently because it still contained enough air to make it float. Soon, the sacking would become waterlogged and sink to the bottom. But when Shep saw it, it was sailing slowly past on the ebbing tide, only a yard or so out from the shore.

"Wonder what's inside?" thought Shep. "Could be bones." He considered for a moment because he never did anything in a hurry, and then slowly and carefully he waded into the river and seized the end of the sack with his teeth. Then he gave a violent start and let go of it, because somebody inside the sack started to cry!

"Oh my dear life!" he gasped, and grabbed hold of the sack again. The crying sank to a hiccuping sob and a tiny voice said:

"Want to get out!"

Shep was unable to reply because his mouth was full of sack, but he struggled back to the shore as quickly as he could, the swollen sack trailing behind. As soon as it was safely on dry land he dropped it and stood panting, the river water streaming off his long, silky coat.

The sack heaved violently and the little squeaky voice cried again:

"Want to get out!"

"All right, all right, bide still while I chew through the string," said Shep soothingly and he set to work with his strong white teeth on the tarry string which was tied tightly round the mouth of the sack. It yielded at last, and as the sack fell open he thrust his long nose within. His muzzle touched something soft, which yelped.

"Ow!" said the little voice. "Don't poke. We're coming out."

The two small figures which crept out of the sack were the most pathetic objects Shep had ever seen, and his tender heart swelled with pity. They were puppies, and if they had been dry they would have been fluffy, but their coats were clinging to their small, thin bodies, their tails were wisps of wetness and their large ears, plastered with mud, dripped dismally. In spite of the warmth of the day both puppies shivered as they looked up at Shep out of round, terrified eyes.

"W-ell!" said Shep slowly. "Well, young shavers, and whatever in the world have you been up to?"

"It wasn't us," said the larger of the two.

"Not us," echoed the smaller faintly, and sneezed.

"He put us in a bag," said the first puppy.

"And threw us away," chimed in the second. She crept nearer to Shep and cuddled into the warmth of his coat. It reminded Shep of new born lambs and his heart simply melted.

"Come to old Shep then," he crooned, and with his long, warm tongue he set to work to lick the puppies clean and dry. They whimpered and whined, rolling over to let him get at their under-neaths, wriggling as he wobbled them backward and forward with the energy he was putting into his work.

At last, dry and clean, they sat up and looked at him anxiously through fringes of long, white hair.

They were pretty puppies, though no one could possibly have told what mixture of breeds had gone into their make-up. Their ears were pure spaniel, but their faces had a sharp, terrier look and their coats, black and white and fluffy, might have belonged to a Pomeranian. Their legs were shortish and their feet enormous. Their tails, now that they were clean and dry, curved over their backs like teapot handles and their little eyes were very dark and bright.

"You poor lil' toads!" said Shep. "Someone tried to drown you, eh? There, there!" he added hastily as the two little creatures began to whimper again. "It's all over now and you're safe with old Shep. Are you hungry?"

The puppies' whimpers grew louder.

"Can you eat?" asked Shep anxiously.

" 'Course we can!" said the larger puppy indignantly.

"Soft things," added the smaller one more

cautiously. "We haven't got many teeth yet." She opened her little pink mouth wide and Shep saw with horror and indignation that the tiny white milk teeth had only just come through.

"Why, you're no more than a month old!" he exclaimed. "You ought to be with your mommy!"

The puppies looked up at him trustfully, still shivering in spite of the warmth of the sun.

"I don't rightly know what to do with you," mumbled Shep, scratching his ear thoughtfully.

"Can't we go home with you?" asked the larger puppy. "Have you got a nice, kind owner?"

"That's the trouble, my little love," said Shep. "I've got no owner at all. I belongs to a gang, see? A gang of homeless dogs that looks after themselves. It's no life for puppies, that's certain."

The smaller puppy gave a little skip in the air. "It sounds wonderful!" she said excitedly. "Tod, doesn't it sound fabulous?"

"Hey!" exclaimed Shep in alarm. "Calm down. What do you think Mike's going to say if I come back with you two? He doesn't run a babies' home you know!"

"Who's Mike?" demanded the larger puppy whose name appeared to be Tod.

"Mike's the leader of the gang," Shep told them.

"Is he nice?" demanded the smaller puppy. Tod called her Tiny, and it seemed to Shep to be a very good name.

"He's the best fellow in the world," said Shep proudly. "And Boston Bill is the cleverest, and Tizzy—" he stopped short and thought for a moment. Then he went on, "There's Tizzy. Now she's a lady and all ladies like babies, so I reckon Tizzy would like you. Why didn't I think of that before?"

"Is Tizzy nice?" asked Tiny hopefully.

"Would she be like our mommy?" demanded Tod.

"Yes, in a way," said Shep.

"Is she furry?" asked Tod.

"Well, no. She's kind of smooth," admitted Shep.

"Our mommy was furry," said Tiny and her voice sounded unsteady. "You could burrow right into her lovely furry coat."

"I don't like smooth ladies," put in Tod, and his ears drooped in a melancholy way.

"Oh dear, oh dear!" groaned Shep. "Now see here, my little love, I'm furry, aren't I?"

"Yes, but you're not a – a – l-lady," wept Tod.

"That don't make a scrap of difference, not in the circumstances," said Shep. "You can cuddle up to me and I'll pretend to be your daddy. How's that, eh?"

"That 'ud be nice," said Tiny, looking up at Shep through her fringe of hair.

"But Tizzy'll have to tell you what to eat and all that," added Shep hurriedly. "That's a job for a lady, that is. I've never had anything to do with little 'uns before, excepting lambs."

"What's lambs?" asked Tod, but Shep said hurriedly, "Tell you later. I've got to get back now or the others'll think I'm lost. And it's long past your bedtime too."

The puppies were so small they found it very hard to keep up with Shep as he left the little beach by the lane which ran past the entrance to the wharf. Their tiny legs ached and their breath came short but no word of complaint passed their lips. They were afraid all the time that Shep would change his mind and shoo them away, and that would be too dreadful.

Shep trotted along until he came to the loose board upon which he scratched softly with his foot. Tizzy's voice from the other side whispered, "Who goes there? Friend or foe?"

"Friend," Shep whispered back.

"Password?"

"Rotten Rats!" said Shep and Tizzy giggled.

"You've got it wrong *again*!" she said. "It's Mouldy Mice!"

"Well, let me in anyway, Tiz," said Shep. "I've – er – I've got something here, something that'll interest you."

"What is it?" asked Tizzy curiously, and pushing the plank aside she peered out. When she saw the puppies she let out a shrill yelp of surprise.

"My stars!" she exclaimed. "Wherever did you find them, Shep?"

"Fished 'em out of the river," said Shep. "Tiz, what do you think Mike will say?"

Tiz stared at him in surprise. "You weren't thinking of bringing them to join the gang, were you?" she demanded. "You must be out of your mind!"

"Well, I can't leave 'em standing in the street," said Shep desperately, and at the sound of his words the twins set up a howl.

"Bring them in quick, for goodness' sake!" said Tiz. "You'll have the police down on us in a minute." Shep pushed the two puppies through the gap with his long nose and squeezed in after them

Boston Bill and Mike were still ratting; that is to say they were sitting back on their haunches by the largest hole exchanging personal remarks with the rats. When they heard the commotion caused by the entrance of Shep and the twins, they both turned around to see what was going on and their eyes nearly popped out of their heads as Shep nudged Tiny and Tod into the middle of the wharf.

"Well I'll be . . . !" said Boston Bill. "A couple of kids! How about that?"

Mike's face set in stern lines. He got up in silence and stalked stiff-legged over to the puppies, and, still silent, stood looking down at them. The twins, terrified, threw themselves on to their backs. Their short legs stuck up stiffly and the last rays of the setting sun shone on their wrinkled pink tummies. They looked so funny that Mike's stern face relaxed in a wide grin. His ears stuck out sideways and his tail began to wag.

"Orphans?" he inquired, and Shep said:

"Well, sort of. Someone tried to—" He came close to Mike and whispered in his ear. Mike scowled.

"Only what I'd expect of owners," he grunted. "Boston Bill, what do you think we ought to do with these kids? A bit young to belong to a gang, eh?"

"They'll grow," said Bill, sauntering up to the group. "Kind of cute, aren't they? Sign 'em on as mascots, Mike. Maybe they'll bring us luck."

6 : Prince

It really was hard luck for Mike. He wanted so badly to be the leader of a rough, tough gang and instead he found himself going off alone on adventures, while all the rest stayed at home fussing over the two puppies. Shep was the worst; he just doted on Tiny and Tod, but Tizzy was nearly as bad, and as for Boston Bill, you would have thought he was their grandfather the way he carried on.

It wasn't that Mike didn't like the twins, he did. He thought they were spunky little tykes and lots of fun, but they weren't gangsters, and never would be, the way they were being spoiled by Bill, Tizzy and soft old Shep. So he took to going off alone and staying away for longer and longer periods, and it was during this time that he met a very aristocratic Chihuahua* called Chiquita and fell deeply in love with her. When she passed out of his life he felt as if his heart would break, but he got over it in the end, although always remembering her kindly.

* *The Smallest Dog on Earth.*

The year wore on and winter arrived with cold rains and frosty nights. It wasn't so comfortable on the old wharf now, but they managed pretty well on the whole. The puppies grew rapidly and were soon able to forage for food, aided by one of the older dogs, who told them what was good to eat and what was not. Shep declared proudly that the kids promised to become the most skilled bin tippers in all London, and they were also extremely good at holding their own with cats.

It was through the twins that another dog came to join the gang. They had been out alone for once, garbaging behind the High Street shops, early in the morning, before the bins were emptied. Tod found a whole stale chocolate cake in the baker's bin. Being young and having a sweet tooth, he ate most of it before he began to feel sick, and stopped. Tiny was wiser. She went for the butcher's bin and breakfasted very well on a large pork chop which had been thrown away by mistake. Neither pork chops nor chocolate cake are really suitable things for puppies, but they did not know any better. When Shep heard what they had eaten he was very worried, but by then it was too late.

Mike and the rest slept late that morning, which was why the twins had managed to slip out alone, and they only woke up when the two puppies came bundling through the hole in the fence, obviously bursting with news. They rushed across the wharf to the packing cases and barrels where the other dogs were still snoozing, yelping excitedly.

"Belt up!" muttered Mike in a drowsy voice.

The twins both began to talk at once, a jumble of sound out of which emerged the words – "poor dog", "car", and "policeman".

"What's that?" asked Mike, suddenly alert. "Did you say something about a policeman?"

"He tried to catch him!" shouted Tod.

"The car never stopped!" chimed in Tiny.

"The poor dog is *awful* hurt," screamed Tod.

"Awful hurt!" echoed Tiny.

"Now wait a minute," drawled Boston Bill. "Calm down, you two, and let's sort this thing out. Tod, you tell us."

"Slowly, dear," put in Tizzy. "What dog is hurt?"

"You never did ought to have gone out alone," said Shep reprovingly. "Haven't I told 'e—"

"Never mind that now," said Mike. "Carry on, Tod."

"*Well!*" said Tod breathlessly. "The car came around the corner and it knocked the poor dog—"

"What dog?" interrupted Tizzy. "Do begin at the beginning, Toddy dear."

"I *am*!" said Tod. "The car came around the corner—"

"It was a green car," put in Tiny. "It came ever so fast."

"What the car was like is neither here nor there," said Bill. "It's the dog that matters."

"He's black," said Tiny. "And the policeman was blue."

"All policemen are blue!" retorted Tod. "Tell them something they don't know."

"Look," said Mike as patiently as he could. "That doesn't matter. The question is, where's the dog?"

"Outside the fence!" said both puppies together.

"Well, why couldn't you have said so to begin with?" snapped Mike. "Shep, go and have a look, there's a good fellow. But watch out for the policeman."

"*He* isn't there," said Tod.

"We shook him off," Tiny told him proudly.

Shep went over to the loose board, pushed it aside and thrust his long head through the gap. Then he gave an exclamation of dismay which made all the other dogs hurry over to join him.

Outside in the lane lay a large Labrador retriever. His eyes were closed, and from a deep cut over one eye blood dripped on to his sleek black coat. He hardly seemed to be breathing and for one dreadful moment Shep thought he was dead. But then the stranger opened his eyes, saw Shep, and with a desperate effort struggled to his feet.

"W-where am I?" he stammered.

"With friends," said Shep quickly. "Come on in, old fellow. Whatever happened to you?"

"We told you – he was hit by a car!" exclaimed Tod impatiently.

"And then the policeman came and—"

"Pipe down, you two," said Mike sternly. "You talk too much."

"Well, I like that!" muttered Tiny. "We found him, didn't we?"

"Hush, dear," murmured Tizzy.

"Won't hush!" said Tiny. "If it hadn't been for us, the policeman would have got him."

"Might have been better if he had," said Bill thoughtfully. "The poor guy looks like a hospital case to me."

"But – but Mike says policemen are *horrible*!" stammered Tiny. "Are they horrible or aren't they?"

"Depends on whether you've got an owner or not," grinned Bill. "Now, out of the way, you kids, and let's get this poor chap in."

The big black dog limped painfully across the wharf and sank down on the straw inside the largest box. All the others stood around anxiously, wondering what to do.

"How do you feel now?" asked Tizzy at last.

"Thirsty," murmured the dog, and he began to pant, his long red tongue hanging out of the side of his mouth.

"There's a good puddle just over there," said Mike. "Think you can make it, chum?"

The Labrador got shakily to his feet, lurched over to the puddle and lapped eagerly. The water seemed to do him good, for he looked around as if seeing the others clearly for the first time and said:

"Thanks very much indeed. You're all very kind. I hope I'm not being a bother."

"Lovely manners," murmured Tizzy approvingly to Bill, who nodded.

"What happened to you?" asked Mike. "These kids said something about the police? We don't want any trouble here—"

"There'll be no trouble," said the black stranger positively. "Why should there be?"

"You haven't – done anything?" inquired Mike. "You're not on the run?"

"No, no, nothing like that," the Labrador assured him. "Do you mind if I lie down again? I'm feeling a bit shaky still. You see, I fell out of the back of my master's car and another car came along and hit me."

"And your master drove on and left you there?" exclaimed Mike indignantly. "I always said owners were no good."

"You've got it wrong," the Labrador told him wearily. "By the way, let me introduce myself. The name's Prince. I'm a gun dog from Sussex, and I came up to London in my master's car, sitting in the back as I usually do. It's an open sports model, very fast." He paused and Bill said curiously:

"How did you happen to fall out?"

Prince looked embarrassed.

"You'll think that I am very badly trained," he said. "The trouble is I can't stand cats."

"Oh, they're not so bad," said Mike. "But I don't see the connection?"

"A cat made fun of me as we drove along that street where your little friends found me, and I – well – I leaned over the back a bit too far, telling it what I thought of it, you know, and the next thing I knew I was on the road. A car came along and ran into me I suppose, because after that I don't remember anything until your two pups arrived. And of course my master drove on, not knowing I'd gone."

"How awful!" said Tizzy. "Do you know where your master was going?"

Prince shook his head. "No idea," he said. "He wasn't stopping in London, just passing through on our way up north somewhere. He may go for miles before he realizes I'm not there. I'm afraid I'm lost."

"Was he a good master?" inquired Shep.

"The very best," said Prince quietly. He turned away and laid his head wearily on his paws. "If I can't find him, I think my heart will break."

There was an uncomfortable silence; no one knew what to do or say. At last Tizzy went up to him and nudged him gently with her nose, and he gave her a grateful look. Shep was unashamedly sniffing and Boston Bill cleared his throat noisily. Only Mike stared out across the river with a hard look on his face. He didn't believe in good masters and thought Prince was making it up.

"Look – er – Prince," he said. "If you're lost you'd better stay with us and join the gang. The only other thing you can do is go and hang around in the street until the police pick you up and then you'll be sent to a Dogs' Home."

"But my address is on my collar!" exclaimed Prince excitedly, and then he gave a little moan of dismay, "Oh dear, I haven't got it on. Master meant to put it on before we started this morning and then he forgot. I don't wear it at home because I never go out alone."

"What – never?" exclaimed Mike, and Prince

said simply, "Never, Master and I are always to-gether."

"How beautiful!" said Tizzy softly. "I've dreamed of having an owner like that."

"Me too," said Shep.

"You're all soft!" exclaimed Mike disgustedly. "What's the good of me trying to run a gang when all you care about is finding owners? I'm fed up with all of you!"

"*We* don't want owners," piped up Tod. "Do we, Tiny?"

"You're only pups," growled Mike, and slouched off to the other end of the wharf where he sat brooding, with his back turned to the rest. He wouldn't let them know it for the world, but there had been something in Prince's eyes when he said "the very best" that had upset Mike a great deal. Suppose that he was wrong after all and there was such a thing as a good owner? Suppose that some-where there was a boy of about fourteen who loved dogs, especially mixed breed dogs who looked a bit like a cairn but not quite; a boy who liked ratting and throwing sticks in the river for people to fetch out, a boy who stroked a dog's ears, and rubbed a dog's chest, and found a corner for a dog on his bed at night; a boy who loved his dog very much indeed and was with him all the time? That would be wonderful, that would, thought Mike wistfully, gazing over the river. Then he grinned sourly and gave himself a shake. Fairy tales – that's all it was. Stuff for kids.

Prince stayed on with the gang until the cut on his head healed up and he stopped limping. During that time Bill and Tizzy and Shep took turns bringing food for him; and the twins, who looked upon him as their special property because it was they who had found him, spent hours playing near him to keep him company. Prince told them stories about the grand house he lived in down in Sussex and all about shooting parties, which excited them very much. The rats got fed up with them at this time because the puppies kept rushing up to their holes and shouting "Bang bang!" The rats complained that it gave them headaches, and was silly anyway.

Mike was always a bit stiff with Prince, but he wouldn't turn him away from the wharf, not even when Prince was quite well again, because he was a kind-hearted dog and could see plainly that the Labrador, big though he was, had no idea how to look after himself. So Prince stayed on and on, always polite and sweet-tempered, but so sad that it brought tears to Tizzy's eyes just to look at him.

"He's such a perfect gentleman," she said. "I can't bear to see him so unhappy. Isn't there any way we could help him to find his master, Bill?"

Bill considered. "It's quite a problem," he said. "If only we could read we might see a notice offering a reward for his return. The police would know of course, but—"

"Oh don't let's bring the police into this!" said Tizzy hastily. "They'd start asking questions and then we'd all be in trouble."

"Don't really see what we can do, honey," said Bill. "Maybe things will work out one day."

"He eats hardly anything at all," mourned Tiz. "Sometimes I think he'll die if his master doesn't find him soon."

She sighed, and began to scrabble together some torn newspapers, which the workmen had left behind, to make a warmer bed. One piece of newspaper was caught up by the wind and blown off the wharf into the river where it floated away on the tide. On the paper was printed in large letters:

LOST, LABRADOR RETRIEVER,
answers to name of Prince.
£10 REWARD.

What a pity that dogs can't read.

7 : The Raid

Christmas was coming, and in the grand parts of London all the streets were decorated with lights, and the shop windows were full of wonderful things for people to eat and wear and to buy as presents. Even in the poorest districts every little shop had a few paper streamers or a little Christmas tree. Small boys went around singing carols, and on the wharf Tiny and Tod trotted up and down chanting:

"Christmas is coming and the geese are getting fat,
  Please to put a biscuit in the old dogs' hat."

They both thought this was very funny, but the older dogs soon had enough of it and told them to be quiet.

The weather got colder and colder. Boston Bill and Prince, who had smooth coats and were used to good living, suffered a great deal. Tizzy was smooth too, but had never been spoiled so she didn't feel the cold as much, and Shep simply loved it. Sheep dogs like dry, frosty weather very much. The puppies grew enormous woolly coats so that they looked like dirty little bears, and as for Mike, his life had always been hard and uncomfortable so he never gave the cold a thought. Besides, his mind was entirely taken up with a Grand Plan.

The Plan was nothing less than a tremendous raid on the garbage cans at the Ritz Hotel, the routing, once and for all, of every cat in that area in order to bring back to the wharf enough food for a tremendous Christmas feast.

Mike made up his mind that everyone, even the puppies, should take part in this raid and behave for once like a real gang. So one night, about a week before Christmas Day, he called a council of war.

"Now look here, everyone," he said. "It's high time we did something adventurous, something worthy of the name of gangsters. Some of you – and I name no names – are a bit soft, and it just won't do."

"I'm not soft!" shouted Tod. "I'm as strong as – as anything, and I'm getting my second teeth."

"The less said about that the better," Tizzy

warned him. "When your second teeth are through you'll be due for a licence and you'll have to watch out for the police."

"Who cares about silly old policemen?" said Tod. "If a policeman came near me I'd – I'd—"

"You'd what?" asked Bill with a grin.

"I'd bite him in the leg!"

"Don't be silly, dear," said Tizzy. "Dogs who bite policemen come to a bad end."

"Do bird dogs have to hold a licence?" inquired Boston Bill, turning to Prince.

"Bird dogs?" said Prince looking puzzled.

"Sorry, forgot I was talking to a Britisher. Gun dogs, then. Do they?"

"Oh yes, indeed, I think so," said Prince. "It's really only the working chaps who don't."

"Like me," said Shep.

"Exactly, old boy. Oh, and the Guide Dogs for the Blind. Splendid fellows."

"A great many of them are ladies," put in Tizzy pointedly. "I am told they learn much more quickly."

Everybody began to talk at once and Mike had to shout to make himself heard.

"If I might be allowed to get a word in!" he yelled. "I was talking about the Plan!"

"You're not thinking of doing anything – er – against the law, I hope?" asked Prince anxiously. "I mean to say, old boy, that wouldn't be quite the thing, would it?"

"It won't be against the law," Mike told him. "But it certainly will be against the cats."

"Oh in that case, count me in," said Prince.

"Us too!" shouted the twins.

"Hush, dears," said Tizzy. "Uncle Mike is trying to make a speech."

"Why the Ritz bins?" asked Bill. "Why not Buckingham Palace? Rich pickings there, I'll bet."

Mike looked shocked.

"That would be disloyal," he said. "Besides there are always people on guard."

"*I* think the Tower of London," suggested Tizzy. "Just think what the Beefeaters must throw away!"

"I said the Ritz Hotel and I mean the Ritz Hotel," put in Mike firmly. "And why? Because there's a gang of cats there led by a character called One-eared Charley who thinks he owns the place, and

I'm going to teach him a lesson. You know him, don't you, Bill?"

"That's so," said Bill. "He's a wise guy, Charley is. It wouldn't do any harm to rough him up a bit."

"Bang bang!" yelled Tod. "Got 'im! Bang bang!"

"Don't you be too hard on the pussies now," said Shep anxiously. "I've known many a nice cat down on the farm."

"There's good cats and bad cats," said Mike. "I was once very fond of a cat myself, but that Charley and his gang – they're bad 'uns."

"They'd scratch your eyes out as soon as look at you," agreed Boston Bill.

"Now listen everybody," said Mike. "This is what we do. Tomorrow night there's a full moon. The kitchen porters put the bins out last thing, ready for emptying next morning, so we'll leave it as late as possible, but not too late or the cats will have picked out all the best stuff. Bill, you'll be in charge of one party with Tiz and Shep, and you'll hide in a doorway at one end of the street. Prince, you'll come with me, and you two kids can be in my party too."

"Hurrah!" shouted the twins.

"Never mind about hurrah," said Mike. "Just you remember to keep your mouths shut and do exactly as you're told. If you don't, you're out of this gang, and I mean *out*."

"We won't make a sound," promised Tiny in a subdued voice. "Only, please Mike, may I bite a cat with my new teeth?"

"If you're good," said Mike. "We'll be hiding at the other end of the street and as soon as the bins are out and Charley and his gang are inside them – we strike! I bet those cats will be so rattled to have us coming at them from both sides that they'll run for their lives, but if they show fight – well, we'll be ready for them."

"I say, old man, do you think that's quite sporting?" asked Prince. "I don't like cats any more than you do, but dash it all, they won't stand a chance."

Mike smiled grimly. "It's easy to see you've had no experience with town cats," he said. "They fight with everything they've got and it takes a brave dog to face them. Watch out for your eyes, everyone. Keep your heads down and go in low. Now!

Everyone off to bed. We'll need to be fresh for tomorrow's work."

The next day dragged by slowly. It was a Sunday, so no workmen came on to the wharf and the dogs were able to rest all day. The older ones dozed most of the time, but Tizzy and the twins were nervous and bored and the day seemed to stretch out until it was as long as a week. At nine o'clock they had a light meal of scraps they had brought in the day before, and some of them went down to the little beach to drink. The sky was clear and glittering with stars and the great, pale moon shone through the frosty air. From all over London church clocks chimed the quarters and the hours and the distant hum of traffic died away to a murmur. On the wharf the rats came out and scuttled down to the water's edge to scavenge for food, slipping silently past the dogs like shadows. Cats appeared, stalking across the rooftops, fighting occasionally with shrill yowls and spitting sounds. Far away a train whistled, and from the dark Thames came a chug-chugging as the long, black launch of the river police went by.

At last Mike whispered, "Now!" and silently the

raiding party set forth, their hearts beating a little faster as the moment of combat drew near. Mike led the way with Shep, then came Boston Bill, with the twins keeping very close to his comfortingly sturdy form, then Tizzy, with big black Prince bringing up the rear. On silent feet they trotted purposefully through the almost deserted streets, taking cover in dark doorways if anyone approached, until they came to the street at the rear of the huge, grand hotel.

They were just in time. As they took up their positions as planned, the doors opened and men came out with the garbage cans, a long row of them all full of exciting possibilities. The men put them down against the wall and disappeared, thankful to have the day's work done.

For a moment there was silence and emptiness and then, suddenly, the cats appeared. They seemed to come from every nook and cranny in the street, black cats, tabby cats, ginger cats, white cats, lean and hungry and savage cats, with torn ears and glaring, angry green eyes. They were part of the great army of London's strays; cats who had never had an owner or known the comfort of a warm bed by a hot fire. These were the cats who had been born on a bomb site or in a ruined house, who had fended for themselves ever since they could walk. These cats were desperate characters and a match for almost any dog.

One-eared Charley led the assault on the bins. He was a black cat with a white shirt front and white feet. He had lost his ear in a fight when he was quite young and his thin body was scarred all over with the marks of battle. He made straight for the nearest bin, knocked the lid off with a clatter and dived within. The other cats followed his example and the iron lids went clang – clatter – clang all along the quiet street.

"They'll wake the whole street!" muttered Prince in dismay, and sure enough a window up above was thrown open and an angry voice shouted:

"Scat! Get out, you brutes!"

The cats froze into silence until the window closed, and then the scuffling and the crunching and the rattling began again. Mike stuck his head out of the cover of the doorway where he was hiding and signalled to Boston Bill.

"*Now!*"

With a rush the dogs advanced from either side and the cats, taken unawares, popped startled faces out of the bins, whiskers bristling and every hair on their bodies on end. The dogs, carried away by excitement, yelped and growled and barked, knocking over the tall bins with a shattering clatter and sending garbage all over the road.

"Up lads and at 'em!" yelled Mike, overcome with the excitement of the chase. He made a rush at One-eared Charley who stood at bay, the most blood-curdling sounds coming from his throat. Then, at the sight of so many dogs, his nerve broke, and he turned and fled, with Mike in hot pursuit.

In a matter of seconds every cat had gone, though not before Tod had received a nasty scratch on the nose, and Tizzy was whimpering from the pain of a torn ear. Boston Bill, wheezing desperately, fought for breath, and Prince, the hair on his back standing up stiffly, muttered something about "cads" under his breath.

All around them on the ground, spilled from the bins, lay the rich remains of luscious meals from the kitchens of the Ritz. But almost before anyone

could grab so much as a chop bone, lights flicked on all up and down the street, windows were flung open and a hail of old shoes and other hard objects descended upon the victorious raiding party.

"Get out of here!" shouted angry voices, and a bucket of icy cold water sloshed into poor Shep's face.

"Call the police!" yelled another voice and someone replied, "Don't bother. Here come the coppers now."

The gang didn't wait to hear any more. With one accord they took to their heels and ran, leaving all the lovely food scattered on the road.

They ran and ran, and behind them they heard the pounding feet of the police! At last the wharf was reached, the loose board pushed aside, and one by one they crept through and collapsed panting on the cold stones of their hideout.

"We've shaken them off," whispered Mike. He got up and stretched, then trotted over to the puddle and took a long drink. "Boy! Did those cats run! It was worth losing the grub to see old One-ear lighting out like that!"

"You promised us a lovely Christmas dinner,"

whined Tiny disconsolately. "And we didn't get anything."

"Never mind, dear," said Tizzy. "Mike will take us on another raid soon, won't you, Mike?"

"Sure, sure," said Mike. "And I'll tell you where we'll go. We'll—"

"Listen!" said Prince tensely, his head cocked on one side. "Somebody's coming."

Everyone froze into silence, and out of the quiet of the night came the sound of boots on paving stones – tramp – tramp – tramp!

The dogs crouched low to the ground, their hearts beating wildly. Would the feet go on past the wharf, or would they – stop? Tramp – tramp – tramp!

Then the loose board was pushed aside by an unseen hand and the bright light of an electric torch roved over the silent group of dogs.

"There's a whole bunch of 'em in there," called a gruff voice. "I'll stay on guard, Bert, while you go and get the dog van!"

8 : Hopes and Homes

"My word, you've brought in a mixed bunch this time," said the kennel man at the Dogs' Home as the policeman opened the back door of the van. "Poor creatures, to think of them being out on their own in this bitter weather."

"They don't look as if they'd done badly for themselves," said the policeman thoughtfully. "They aren't thin, and we got on to them because they made such an uproar upsetting the bins behind the Ritz Hotel. Those two pups are as fat as little pigs."

"Fat yourself!" muttered Tod, but fortunately for him the policeman didn't understand.

"They all seem to be friends, so we'll put 'em in one big kennel for what's left of tonight and sort them out in the morning," said the kennelman. "I do feel sorry for these strays, I really do. A dog needs an owner. Cats get on all right, but dogs want someone to love."

"That's what *you* think," growled Mike.

"He could be right," said Tizzy wistfully.

"He *is* right," pronounced Prince.

"Come on then, my beauties, out you come!" said the kennelman, and the dogs left the van and followed him along a corridor which smelled strongly of disinfectant, into a big kennel with a concrete floor and a bench piled high with clean straw. It looked inviting, and Shep jumped up on it and lay down. He was still wet from the water which had been thrown over him and he rolled in the straw to dry himself. Bill, wheezing worse than ever, lay down beside him, and the twins, who had never seen such quantities of straw in their lives, yelped excitedly and burrowed into it like moles. Tizzy joined them, but Prince remained standing at the wire door, lost in a dream of hope that perhaps now he was in a Home his master would find him. Mike lay down on the concrete floor, his back turned to everyone else and his head on his paws.

"Come to bed, Mike, old friend," said Bill coaxingly.

Mike made no reply. He felt bitterly that all the others had let him down. Not one of them seemed to be upset at having been captured and brought to this place. Not one of them had made the slightest effort to escape. They had just filed into the van like a silly flock of sheep, and now they were settling down to sleep as happily as if they were still in their hideout on the wharf. Gangsters! Mike gave a hollow laugh. There wasn't a true gangster among them. All they really wanted was owners, and it looked as if that was what they were going to get.

But not him! Oh no! No owner for Mike!

The kennelman came back with food, and everyone, except Mike, ate it eagerly. It was now three o'clock in the morning and they were hungry, having saved up for the wonderful meal they had hoped to have at the Ritz.

Mike ate nothing. The kennelman tried to coax him, but he just stayed curled up in a tight, miserable bundle, pressed against the wall. At last the man gave up trying and stood looking at the other dogs thoughtfully. His eye stayed longest on Prince, and presently he took a printed paper out of his pocket and read it carefully. Then he said aloud:

"Thought so! You're on the list of lost dogs, my

boy. We'll contact your owner in the morning and you'll soon be home."

"Oh, thanks most awfully, my man," said Prince, but the kennelman just thought he was wagging his tail.

"As for the rest of you – well – we'll have to see what we can do. You seem friendly, all except the little grouch in the corner there. We ought to be able to find owners for everyone, except him."

"I wouldn't take an owner as a gift," muttered Mike. "Just give me half a chance and I'll be out of here and you'll never catch me again." He showed his teeth at the kennelman who shook his head sorrowfully and said:

"It's a pity about you, old chap. No one wants a bad-tempered dog. Well, sleep tight all. See you in the morning."

Then he put out the light and went away.

"Oh Prince, aren't you lucky?" sighed Tizzy in the darkness.

"By Jove, yes, I should say I am!" said Prince. "I can hardly wait to see my old Master. Not that it hasn't been very jolly with all you dear people," he added hastily in case he had hurt their feelings. "But a dog needs an owner, no doubt of that."

"The right owner," put in Boston Bill.

"Of course, that goes without saying," agreed Prince.

"I would dearly love to go back to the country," said Shep longingly.

"I'm getting a bit old for the roving life," mused Boston Bill. "If I could find an owner who'd just stay quiet in one place without all this travelling around—"

"Traitors!" hissed Mike, but no one seemed to hear him.

"I think I'd like a lady owner," said Tizzy. "A nice lady who lives in a nice house with a nice little garden. I'd like to better myself, I would."

The twins said nothing, because they were both fast asleep.

Next morning the dogs were let out into a big yard for exercise. Mike tried hard to find a way of escape, but the Dogs' Home was used to people who wanted to escape and knew all the ways of preventing it. There wasn't a hope, and Mike told himself that he would just have to wait until they handed him over to someone, and then give them the slip as soon as possible. He refused to talk to any of the gang, but he did have a few words with some of the other dogs in the yard. He soon found, however, that every one of them was living in hopes of being found by their owners or adopted by somebody nice. Not one single dog in the whole place seemed to feel as he did, that a chap could get on very well on his own.

Prince was the first of the gang to leave the Dogs' Home. His owner called for him soon after midday and when Prince saw him his joy was so great he very nearly broke down. But he managed to control himself and walked away down the long corridor, keeping strictly to heel.

"Beautiful!" sighed Tizzy when he had gone. "Oh, I do admire these highly trained types!"

"You make me sick," growled Mike.

Late in the afternoon the kennelman came down the passage followed by a little, round woman, with a plump, cheerful face and a calm, placid manner. She stopped at the barred door of the kennel and peered through it intently. Then she beckoned to the man and said, "That little fat, smooth one there – what about him?"

"He's a bit old, ma'am," said the kennelman doubtfully. "Well bred, you know, but getting on a bit."

"So am I," said the little woman cheerfully. "I think we might suit each other very well. Could we have him out?"

"Certainly, ma'am," said the kennelman, and opening the door he snapped his fingers at Boston Bill. "Come on, old chap," he said.

The plump little woman looked at Bill carefully, and Bill looked back at her. She was about as different from his last owner as chalk from cheese and he thought she might suit him very well.

"I need a dog to keep me company," said the little woman. "I live very quietly and never go away from home, and I can't walk far, so I don't want a dog who needs a lot of exercise. I think this one might be just right for me."

"I'm beginning to think the same thing myself," said Boston Bill. "Someone who never goes away and never stays in hotels is just what I want. I did think I'd like to go home to the States to end my days, but I'll settle for a Britisher if she's the right sort." He wagged his stumpy tail and the little woman smiled.

"I fancy he likes me," she said. "What sort of dog is he? An American Boston bull terrier? Well, isn't that nice? I've been in America in my younger days. I was a lady's maid and I travelled a lot. We'll have something to talk about, won't we, old chap? Are you coming with me?"

"Sure!" said Boston Bill, and then he too walked down the long corridor and was gone.

"Oh dear me!" sighed Tizzy. "I wonder who'll be next?"

"Us, I expect," said Tod. "People like puppies, don't they? I'm awfully excited. Tiny's excited too."

"Want to stay with you, Tod," said Tiny anxiously.

"Well, of *course*!" said Tod.

"That's what you think," muttered Mike.

All that afternoon people came and went. It was a good time to find homes for dogs as it was near to Christmas. Fathers and mothers came to choose a nice dog to give to the children for a Christmas present; children came to buy one with money they had been given by uncles and aunts, and kind-hearted animal lovers came because it was the time of good-will and they wanted to give a home to some lonely, ownerless stray. It was one of these people who bought Tizzy, and it really seemed as if a fairy godmother must have heard Tizzy describing the sort of home she wanted and decided to make her dream come true. You only had to take one look at Tizzy's new owner to see that she lived in a nice little house with a nice little garden, and that she would buy Tizzy a nice little basket with a comfortable cushion, and a pretty little china bowl with DOG on it, and take her for walks on a pale blue leash. She chose Tizzy because she liked her shiny, smooth coat, so easy to keep clean.

"Good-bye, Mike," said Tizzy wistfully as she was led away, but Mike wouldn't answer. He was still curled up in a tight ball with his back turned to the door and he remained that way all the time.

Next day the twins went. They were bought by a father and mother who had a large family of very jolly children, all of whom longed to keep pets, but had never been able to before because they had lived in a flat, right in the middle of London. But now their father, who was a clergyman, had been moved to a vicarage in the suburbs with a big house and a big garden and he had promised that every child should have a pet for Christmas. One chose a cat, and two chose rabbits and guinea pigs and one wanted a canary most of all. But the other two, a girl and a boy, wanted dogs, and the twins were obviously the very thing.

Off they went, almost hysterical with excitement, and now there was no one left in the big kennel except Shep and Mike, and it was hard to say which of them was the more miserable, Shep because he was afraid he wouldn't get an owner, or Mike because he was afraid he would.

"Not that I'll stay with him if I do," he kept telling Shep defiantly. "Soon as they open the door – off I go!"

Two more days went slowly by. Dogs came in and dogs went out, people came and people went with the dogs they had chosen, but no one came near Shep and Mike except the kennelman and he seemed to look at them more doubtfully with every hour that passed.

"Difficult types to find homes for," Mike heard him mutter as he glanced through the bars of the door.

"Just leave that door open a crack and you won't have to bother about me," retorted Mike, but the man only gave him another long, worried look and went away.

Then, the day before Christmas Eve the two dogs, more anxious now than they cared to admit, heard slow, deliberate footsteps coming down the corridor towards them, footsteps which were surely made by someone wearing hob-nailed boots – country boots. The footsteps stopped outside their kennel, a rosy country face peered in, and a voice said in a broad, Devonshire accent:

"Where be 'ee then, m'dear?"

"What did he say?" Mike whispered to Shep who had got up from the bench and was showing signs of excitement. "Is he a foreigner, do you think?"

"He's a Devon man!" exclaimed Shep. "He said where be – I mean, where is he, then, my dear?"

"Ah, I see 'un now!" exclaimed the Devon man. "He be proper handsome!"

"Aye, he's a good-looking dog," agreed the

kennelman. "Sweet tempered too, not like that other little tyke."

"Could us have 'un out, do 'e think?" inquired the Devon man, and the kennelman opened the door to let Shep through. Quick as a flash Mike tried to slip out too, but the kennelman was up to all the tricks. His foot shot out and pushed Mike gently back into the kennel. The door clanged shut and he was a prisoner again.

"Do you want a sheep dog for work?" the kennelman inquired as the old man looked Shep over admiringly. "We know nothing about this dog. He was brought in as a stray. He may work or he may not."

"Nay, I've no use any more for a working dog," said the old man from Devon. "Leastways, not what a fellow like this would call work. I keep a few sheep on the moor, but more as a hobby than a business. A retired farmer, I am. I lost my old dog a few weeks ago and I must have another, for I feels lost without a dog. I come here because I'm up in London staying with my married daughter and she tells me of all the poor dogs waitin' for homes. Well, ses I, I'm wantin' a dog and somewhere there's a

123

dog wantin' a master, so maybe we could get together. This fine fellow should be back in the country where he belongs. What d'you say, old fellow? Will 'e come with me?"

"Don't be soft, Shep!" called Mike from the other side of the bars. "Think of the glorious freedom we had on the old wharf! Say you won't go!"

But Shep wasn't listening. He had thrust his long nose into the old man's hand, and the old man was chuckling softly and rubbing Shep behind the ears. Then they walked away down the long corridor together, leaving Mike all alone.

Very slowly he walked over to the bench. Listlessly he scrabbled out a nest in the straw and lay down, his back to the door.

It was all over, Mike's gang. Not one of them really wanted to be free. All they wanted was to belong to someone, to give and take love from humans. Every one of them, in spite of knowing only too well that some owners were bad, believed that somewhere there was a good owner, just waiting for them.

For the first time a tiny doubt crept into his mind. Perhaps after all it was true. Perhaps Shep really would be happier with his old man from Devon, and Tizzy with her lady, and Bill with his. Perhaps the twins would have a wonderful time with their large family of children. Perhaps – perhaps somewhere there was a boy of about fourteen who wanted a funny, mongrel dog – but no, that was just a fairy tale. For him, Mike, there was no one at all.

He burrowed deeper into the straw and a low, heartbroken whimper was forced from his throat by his loneliness and sorrow. Why bother to be brave any more? There was no one to see or hear.

Footsteps came down the corridor, light and quick. Mike scarcely heard them, he was so absorbed in his grief. Then he heard the kennelman say, "How much money have you got?" and a boy's voice answered, "Not a lot, I'm afraid. I'll have to keep seven and six for a licence and I've only got ten bob."

The kennelman laughed. "Half a crown!" he said. "You can't expect much of a dog for that."

"I don't mind what sort of a dog it is," said the boy's voice eagerly. "I like a mixture."

Very slowly, Mike uncurled and sat up, and as he

appeared out of the straw he heard the boy give an excited shout.

"That one! That's the one I want! Oh, can I have that one for half a crown?"

Mike looked across at the door and saw a boy of about fourteen with a freckled face and yellow hair which stood up on end. He was dressed in old jeans and a turtle-necked sweater and he looked tough and friendly and kind. He looked to be the sort of boy who would take a dog ratting and throw sticks into the water for him, and love him very, very much, and never leave him for a moment, except when he had to go to school.

The kennelman opened the door and the boy came in. He knelt down by the bench and he tickled Mike behind his ears and rubbed his chest, and Mike put up his head and licked the boy on the nose. Quite suddenly he knew that all the other dogs had been right, and that a *good* owner was the best thing in the world for a dog to have.

Side by side the boy and the dog went down the long corridor, out into the frosty, Christmassy streets – together.